Three Together

igloo

igloo

Published in 2008
by Igloo Books Ltd
Cottage Farm,
Sywell,
NN6 0BJ
www.igloo-books.com

10 9 8 7 6 5 4 3 2 1

ISBN: 978 1 84561 933 6

Cover design by Insight Design
Cover illustrated by © Rachel Ellen Designs Ltd
Interior illustrations by Liz and Kate Pope

Printed and manufactured in China

The Mystery
of the
Secret Swimmer

by Carol Lawrence

igloo

Chapter 1

All Arranged

"It just isn't the same as swimming in the sea!"

"KC, nothing's as good as swimming in the sea. But it's a lot better than no swimming at all!"

"Sorry, Poppy; I didn't mean to complain. It was great of your mum to get us into the swimming club. I just can't forget last summer!"

The summer was over, and nine-year old Poppy, her best friend KC, and Poppy's seven-and-a-half-year old brother, Sam were back at school. The girls had been talking about how much they missed their swimming, ever since they'd got back from visiting Poppy and Sam's aunt, who lived by the beach. Then, one day when Poppy came home from school, her mum had some exciting news.

"I've phoned the sports centre. They're

starting a swimming club after school on Tuesdays and Thursdays, and they have some spare places for children your age. You just have to be able to swim two lengths of the pool before you can join. I'm sure you can do that! What do you think? Would you like to join?"

"Of course I would!" exclaimed Poppy, her green eyes sparkling. "But, Mum, KC would love it, too! Can I ring her and get her to ask her Mum if she can join?"

Soon, it was all arranged. Tuesday was their first day at the swimming club. KC and Poppy were sitting in the lobby of the sports centre, waiting to be picked up from their first session.

"I can't forget the summer, either. But this is better in some ways, KC. Mrs. Hardiman is great. She'll teach us to swim really well – all the right strokes and stuff. And it will be cool if we can do some diving, too! We couldn't do that from the beach."

"I know, and it really is going to be good. I wish Sam

wasn't too young to join the club. He's really jealous!"

When Poppy's mum arrived to pick them up after their first session, Sam was in the car, along with Jasper the dog. Jasper belonged to the family, but Poppy always thought of him as her own special dog. Poppy gave Jasper a big hug, and he licked her on the nose.

"Sorry, girls! The phone rang just as I was coming out," said Poppy's mum.

Sam winked at Poppy. Their mum was always late for everything – but she always had an excuse.

"Can KC come back to our place for a while?" asked Poppy.

"Sorry, Poppy, not tonight. I'd have thought you'd both be tired after all that swimming!"

Poppy wasn't tired at all. She felt she could swim for at least another hour, or even two!

The girls had really enjoyed their first swimming session. They made sure that they didn't miss any of the sessions and, as the weeks went by, their swimming really started to improve.

Mrs. Hardiman had noticed how good Poppy and KC were. They were natural swimmers, though they had a lot to learn. At the end of one of the sessions she called Poppy, KC and two of the boys over.

"I'd like a word with you four after you've changed. Could you meet me in the lobby?" she said.

When the girls got to the lobby, KC's mum had already arrived to give them a lift home. Mrs. Hardiman was waiting there, too.

"Now Poppy, KC, Jerry and Rick - I've been watching you four and I think you've all got real promise. There's a junior swimming competition in a couple of months and I'd like to enter all four of you. It will mean extra coaching, though, and you need to be committed. What do you think?"

"I'd love to!" said Poppy. "What about you, KC?"

"Sure, let's go for it!" KC replied, excitedly.

The boys were enthusiastic, too.

"There's just one thing. It'll mean training sessions before school, starting at 7.30 am, three days a week. Do you think you can you manage that?"

"I could bring you in the mornings," said KC's mum.

"Thanks!" said Poppy. "Don't leave it to my mum – we'd never be on time!"

The first session was on Friday morning. KC's mum made sure Poppy and KC arrived at the sports centre early – and Sam came along so they could all make the short walk to school together after the training session. Sam thought it was a good idea for him to watch the training so he could pick up tips for when he was old enough to join the club.

"Have a great time!" called KC's mum as the three friends got out of the car.

The main door to the sports centre was still locked.

"We'll just have to hang around until someone gets here," said Poppy.

Suddenly, KC heard a whistle from inside the centre.

"Someone's already in there," she said.

They all listened.

"What was that?" asked Sam.

"It was a splash," said Poppy. "What's going on?"

Chapter 2
Someone's Swimming!

"Someone's swimming in there already!" said KC.

"How did they manage that?" questioned Sam. "It's not open yet!"

The pool had clear glass windows, but they were too high for the friends to see through.

"Lift me up, Poppy," said Sam. "I'll look in to see what's going on."

Sam was heavier than he looked, so KC had to help.

"Whatever are you three doing?" asked a voice behind them.

"Oh, hello, Mrs. Hardiman!"

The girls let go of Sam, who slithered to the ground with a thump.

"We just wondered who was swimming in the pool so early in the morning."

"Nobody. The centre doesn't open till 7.30,"

said Mrs. Hardiman, just as the custodian rounded the corner, holding a key ring.

"But there was a lot of splashing going on," explained Poppy.

They all listened, but the splashing had stopped.

"Well, I can't hear it! Maybe you were mistaken! Come on, you three, let's get going. There's a lot to do!"

Mrs. Hardiman started the training session in the same way as she started the swimming club. The four swimmers had a warm-up splash-

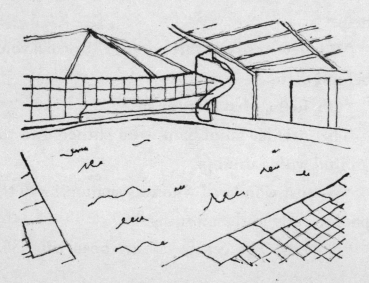

around for a few minutes, then they all got down to business.

Mrs. Hardiman explained the competition that they would be competing in. "The swimming races are two or four lengths of the pool. We are going to start by learning how to turn. You can lose lots of time if you don't turn correctly."

There was a viewing gallery around the pool, and Poppy expected to see Sam sitting there, but there was no sign of him when she looked up. Poppy was worried at first. Where had he gone? Surely he couldn't get into trouble in the sports centre?

Then to Poppy's relief, Sam appeared and waved at her and waved to his sister. Good! Now she could concentrate on the swimming!

As the three friends walked to school afterwards, Sam explained where he'd been.

"Someone was swimming in the pool, whatever Mrs. Hardiman says! So I hung around in the lobby to see who was going out. I went under cover."

"What do you mean, you went under cover?" asked Poppy.

"I pretended to read my book. Books have covers, don't they?"

"Ha ha, very funny! So who did you see?"

"Nobody," replied Sam.

"But I'm sure there was someone in there too. We all heard the noise. Maybe they were hanging around in the sports centre. Did you check the snack bar?" asked KC.

"It's not open till nine o'clock. But I did find out something. The sports centre has got a back door – and when I went there, it was open. And it's one of those doors that only opens from the inside. Someone must have gone out that way."

"I feel a mystery coming on!" said Poppy. There was nothing the three friends liked more than solving mysteries.

"What do we do next?" asked KC.

"Well, I found a place to hide near the back door," said Sam. "If we hear the swimmer again, I'll go there and hide, and see who comes out."

"Don't suppose it's really going to b
though," Poppy said. "Maybe it's just one
lifeguards having a swim before starting work
But you will need to be carcful, Sam."

Sam looked pleased with himself.

"I haven't finished yet. Before I went
to the viewing gallery, I did more
investigating. I looked in the changing
room. There were wet footprints on the
floor – and I found this!"

Sam stuck his hand in his pocket
and pulled out a small silver chain.

"It was on the floor
by the footprints. The
secret swimmer must
have dropped it!"

"Sam, you should
have handed it in at the reception
desk. You know you shouldn't have kept it." said
Poppy.

Sam's face fell. He hadn't thought of that.

KC felt sorry for him. "Don't worry, Sam.

next time," she said. "Or, if _ swimmer, you could give it _ _ r her, or whoever it is."

_ _ _ _ at the chain. It was a very plain _ _ _ _ _ a good luck charm in the shape of the let _ _ _ on it. Could this be a clue?

When they arrived for their next session, the three friends couldn't hear any splashing sounds to be heard. Maybe they had got it wrong, after all.

"As soon as the door opens, go to the reception desk and hand in the chain," Poppy said to her brother.

But Sam had a confession to make. He looked at the floor as he said miserably, "I can't find it! I put it in my school bag to keep it safe, but it's not there any more!"

Poppy groaned. Things were getting complicated!

"I think we're going to have to find out who the swimmer is, if we hear splashing again. Then Sam can say sorry for losing the chain."

Sam didn't look too happy. "Whatever," he

said. But he knew his sister was right.

A few days later, KC telephoned Poppy. Her voice sounded strange.

"What's the matter, KC?" asked Poppy.

"I've caught a cold. I can go to school, but I can't do swimming training tomorrow. I'll have to sit and watch."

"You could hide at the back with Sam. If the secret swimmer comes out, you could go and tell them about the chain."

Sam was relieved. Confessing would be much easier if KC were with him.

The next morning, they arrived at the sports centre and, once again, heard splashing inside the building. The secret swimmer was there again!

When Mrs. Hardiman arrived, they all went inside.

"I'm sorry about your cold, KC. Make sure you come watch. I've got something new to show you today."

KC knew that Mrs. Hardiman would be

expecting to see her in the viewing gallery. She only had a few minutes while the others got changed and warmed up. She tugged at Sam's sleeve.

"Come on Sam, show me your hiding place."

"All right, but don't you give me that horrible cold. I don't want to be all snivelly."

They went to the back of the sports centre.

"There's the door," said Sam.

"Where's your hiding place?" asked KC.

"Just here. See the big bins?" said Sam pointing.

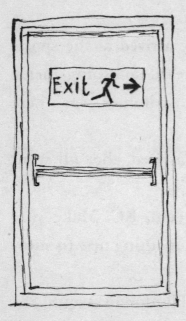

"Sam, those bins are full of garbage. I'm not going to hide in there!"

"Not in the bins, silly. Behind the bins."

"But they smell!" said KC, wrinkling up her nose.

"You have a cold. You won't be able to smell

anything. Quick! The door's opening. Someone's coming out!"

Sam and KC scuttled behind the bins just in time so see a boy come out of the door. He looked like he was a few years older than KC. He was wearing a tracksuit, with a jacket on top. He was carrying a sports bag and was wearing a baseball cap pulled down over his eyes. His jacket collar was turned up. Whoever he was, he didn't want anyone to recognise him.

"Come on, Sam. Let's catch up with him," said KC, curious about this mysterious boy.

They tried to squeeze out from between the

bins at the same time – and got stuck. By the time they had got out, the secret swimmer was nowhere to be seen.

Chapter 3

Not Getting Caught!

KC and Sam rushed to the front of the building. They saw the swimmer going through the main gate of the sports centre and walking up the road towards the centre of town.

"We'll have to let him go, Sam. I need to get to the pool before the training starts, and you can't go into town by yourself."

At the end of the swimming session, KC and Sam met up with Poppy, bursting with their news. They told her what had happened as they walked to school.

"I told Mrs. Hardiman that we'd heard the swimmer again," said Poppy. "Just in case someone told her about it. But she didn't know anything. She said no one is allowed to swim by themselves in the pool, because it's not safe. You always have to have a teacher or a lifeguard there."

"Next time, let's get here really early," said KC. "We can lift Sam up to look in the windows again. Maybe he can see if the swimmer really is that boy we saw coming out the door."

There were no more splashing sounds when the three friends arrived at the next few training sessions. But, one morning, the three friends heard the sound again. "Quick!" said Sam. "Lift me up to the window before anyone comes."

"Ow!" said Poppy, as she and KC hoisted Sam up. "Careful! That was my nose!"

"Sorry!" said Sam. "Anyway, that's not high enough. Push me up a bit more!"

Sam managed to hang on to the frame at the bottom of the big window and pull himself up a little bit more. It was just enough to be able to peep in.

"Hurry up!" said KC. "I can't hold you much longer!"

"OK, let me down," said Sam.

"What did you see?" asked Poppy, eagerly.

But Mrs. Hardiman arrived just at that moment.

"Tell you later," Sam whispered.

"Hello, you three!" said Mrs. Hardiman. "KC, how's that cold of yours?"

"Much better, thanks. Mum says I can do training today."

"Great! Come on then – you've got some catching up to do!"

Poppy and KC couldn't wait to hear what Sam had found out when they were on their way to school.

"It was hard to see what was going on inside because the window was steamed up. But there were two people there. I couldn't really see the swimmer because he was in the water. But the other person was sitting on that lifeguard platform thing watching."

"What did he look like?"

" I couldn't tell whether it was a he or a she. But they were wearing a bright red tracksuit. While you were swimming, I hung around outside the pool, and this woman came out. And guess what? She was wearing a bright red track suit!"

Sam grinned triumphantly.

"Here's the even better bit. She was wearing a name badge – her name's Shelley Carter."

"Sam, that's great detective work, but there's a problem," said Poppy.

"What?"

"All the lifeguards wear red tracksuits. It's the sports centre uniform!"

The three friends knew they were going to have to try harder if they were going to find out anything about the secret swimmer.

At the next training session, there was a big truck parked in front of the sports centre. It was delivering sports equipment, so the doors

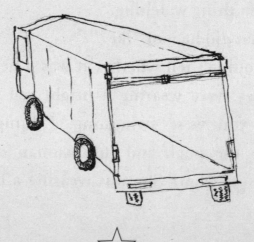

to the pool were wide open. The men who were delivering the items were nowhere to be seen.

"There's the splashing again. Now's our chance to get a look at the secret swimmer!" said Poppy. "We can go up to the viewing gallery. Come on!"

They slipped in through the door and headed for the pool. The corridors were deserted.

Suddenly, a door opened down the corridor and two people came out, both wearing red tracksuits.

☆   ☆   ☆

Chapter 4

He's Brilliant!

Poppy, KC and Sam pressed themselves against the wall of the corridor. They would be in really big trouble if someone saw them.

"Maybe they won't let us come and swim any more," KC thought.

But the two people were so busy talking, they didn't notice the three friends at the end of the corridor. The two talkers turned the other way and disappeared through a door.

"Phew, that was close!" whispered KC.

Poppy quietly opened the door of the viewing gallery. Keeping low, they crept to the balcony and peeped over.

There, in the pool below them, was the boy Sam and KC had seen coming out of the back door. And could he swim!

"Wow! said Poppy. "He's brilliant!"

They knew from their lessons with Mrs.

Hardiman how to move through the water fast. This boy was super fast – and it looked almost as if he wasn't really trying.

The lifeguard was holding a stopwatch. When the boy reached the end of the lane, she called out a time.

Sam looked triumphant.

"See!" he whispered. "It was Shelly Carter."

The swimming session came to an end. The boy climbed out of the water and disappeared into the changing room. Shelley Carter left the pool, and the water gradually settled and became still.

"But what's going on? Why is he swimming in secret?"

"No idea, but I'd really like to find out!" said Poppy. "Come on, KC. It's half past seven. We need to change!"

Mrs. Hardiman's swimming team was good but, even though Sam didn't know much about swimming, he had watched champion swimmers on TV. He knew that nobody in the class came close to being as good as the secret swimmer. This guy was a real champion! Who could he be?

As they walked to school, it was Poppy's turn to look pleased.

"I've found out something," she said. I've found out the swimmer's name!"

"How did you find that out?" asked Sam.

"Mrs. Hardiman was in a hurry to get away this morning, but she had a letter for the person in charge of the sports centre. She asked me to take it to the main office. When I got to there, the secretary was talking on the phone. And, while I was waiting, I saw a timetable for the day up on the wall, so I sneaked a look. And there it was!"

"What?" asked KC.

"The swimmer's name. Between 6:30 and 7:30, the pool is assigned to Shelley Carter and Rob Smith."

KC jumped in. "Well, we know who Shelley

Carter is. The boy has to be Rob Smith. And the chain had a letter 'R' on it!"

"What do we do now?" asked Sam.

They thought, and thought, but couldn't come up with any answers. That evening Sam, who was great on the computer, went online and searched for 'Rob Smith' and 'Rob Smith swimmer'. He found that there were thousands of people in the world called Rob Smith, and too many of them seemed to like swimming! It was hopeless.

The next training day was wet; the sky was a mass of low, grey clouds, and it looked as if it wasn't going to stop raining all day. When Poppy, KC and Sam arrived at the sports centre, there were puddles all over the car park.

"We don't need to go inside!" KC grumbled. "We could practice out here! What a rotten day."

There was a canopy over the front door, and they all huddled underneath it, waiting for the door to open. One by one, the other members of the swimming squad turned up. But where was Mrs. Hardiman?

They heard a key turning in a lock behind them. The lady from the reception desk was opening the door. "Hello!" she said.

They all headed inside. Suddenly, Poppy felt a painful jab in the ribs.

"Ow! What was that for?"

"Look!" hissed KC. "In the car park!"

Rob Smith was walking towards a car that was waiting for him. He must have come out of the back door of the Sports Centre. The car windows were wet, so they couldn't see who was inside. Rob Smith opened the door and the car drove off.

"I've seen that car somewhere before!" said Poppy. "But I can't think where!"

"There are loads of cars like that one," said KC.

Sam took out his notebook.

"What are you doing, Sam?"

"Writing down the licence number," he answered.

Chapter 5

Whose Car?

It rained all morning and the whole school had to stay indoors at recess. Poppy and KC hated being stuck indoors but Sam loved it – he was allowed to use the computer. He tried looking for Rob Smith on the internet again, but without any luck.

Poppy gazed out the window, which overlooked the teachers' car park.

She gasped. That car! She was sure it was the same one they had seen at the sports centre.

She went to find Sam.

"Sam, where's your notebook? I'm sure that car we saw is outside."

Sam rummaged in his school bag. What was that, shining at the bottom of the bag?

Sam held up the missing chain, triumphantly.

"That's great, Sam! It must have slipped through a hole into the lining of the bag," said Poppy.

Sam gave Poppy his notebook, and she rushed back to window.

The trouble was, she couldn't see the licence plate clearly.

By midday, the rain had stopped. Poppy met up with Sam and KC.

"The car! I've seen it! It's in the school car park!" She said excitedly.

KC wasn't convinced. "I told you, there are lots of cars like that," she said.

"Let's look," Sam suggested. "We can see the car park from the end of the yard."

They went to the end of the schoolyard, and peered through the metal fence.

The car parking space was empty!

Just then, another car pulled into the space. A man got out and waved at the three friends looking through the fence.

"Hi, gang. Can you tell me where the school office is?"

"We'll take you there if you like," said Poppy.

The man opened the gate and came through.

He smiled at them.

"I'm teaching a class this afternoon because one of your teachers is going off on a course."

"Which teacher?"

"Miss Smith. Oh, I can see the office now. Thanks for showing me. 'Bye for now!"

"Of course!" said KC. "Miss Smith! She takes the top class!"

"What do you mean?"

"Rob Smith, Miss Smith. S.M.I.T.H. Don't you see?" asked KC.

"Just one thing to do," said Sam. "We have to make sure it is the same car. We'll check that out in the morning."

"Then what?" asked KC.

"We'll talk to Miss Smith!" said Poppy.

The next morning, Sam, Poppy and KC crossed the schoolyard and looked through the fence. Miss Smith's car was in its usual place.

"That's the one. The licence plate matches!" said Poppy, excitedly.

Poppy and KC wondered what to do next.

They couldn't just go up to Miss Smith and ask her who the secret swimmer was. But then Poppy remembered that Sam had found the chain. That would be their excuse. They could give it back to her.

At lunchtime, Poppy and KC went to look for Miss Smith.

"The bell for classes will go any minute!" said Poppy.

"Look! She's in the library!" said KC.

The girls went up to the teacher, who smiled at them.

"Hello, Miss Smith," KC said. "We saw you the other day – at the sports centre – picking someone up."

Miss Smith didn't look pleased.

"We think the person you picked up may have dropped something," said Poppy. "Does this chain belong to him?"

Miss Smith looked at it. "Oh, yes! He said

he'd lost it. Thank you very much, girls."

Miss Smith turned away. She obviously didn't want to tell them anything else about the swimmer!

"Poppy and I belong to a swimming club, Miss Smith," KC said. "We're going to be in a swimming competition soon. So we've decided to do a project on swimming. We were wondering if you might know any really good swimmers who could help us?"

Chapter 6
Miss Smith Won't Talk

Miss Smith looked flustered.

"Why are you asking me this? If you need to know about swimming, there are books in the library that can help you."

It wasn't going well, but KC continued.

"We need to interview someone — someone who knows what it's like to be a really good swimmer."

This was getting difficult. Miss Smith obviously didn't want to talk about swimming.

"We noticed that the person you picked up is a really good swimmer," Poppy said, politely.

Miss Smith was looking really annoyed now.

"I'm very busy right now. I was picking up my nephew, who had gone for a swim before school. That's all. Now, there's the bell."

"Sorry, Miss Smith," chorused the two girls.

Poppy and KC told Sam about the conversation

they'd had after school.

"The chain did belong to Rob Smith," Poppy said. "But Miss Smith didn't want to talk about him at all. She said he was swimming before school but we know the sports centre isn't open before half past seven. There's something strange going on."

"At least we know something new. Miss Smith is his aunt. What now?" wondered KC.

"No idea. If Miss Smith won't talk to us, we're stuck!" Poppy replied.

Poppy and KC continued to go to their swimming club twice a week after school, as well as doing the morning training sessions. The morning training was hard work, but the swimming club was fun.

A few days after Poppy and KC had spoken to Miss Smith, the two girls were waiting in the lobby of the sports centre after swimming club. Poppy's mum was picking them up and, for once, she was on time.

"Mum, how about a drink before we go home?

Swimming makes you thirsty," Poppy said.

Poppy's mum smiled. "OK, but we can't be too long, I've got Jasper in the car. You two head along to the snack bar and get yourselves a drink – and one for me too, please! Here's some money. I'll phone KC's mum to say we'll be a bit late."

Poppy and KC went to the snack bar and joined the queue. Suddenly, KC jabbed Poppy in the ribs with her elbow.

"KC, I wish you would stop doing that. It hurts!"

"Never mind that. Poppy, look over there!"

Poppy looked, and gasped. Shelley Carter was sitting at one of the tables, chatting to Miss Smith!

A voice suddenly interrupted them. "What would you like?"

"Three fresh orange juices, please," said Poppy.

"If we sit at the next table, we can listen in to what they're saying," said KC.

"They may notice," said Poppy.

Poppy paid for the drinks and the two girls went to sit down. KC walked past the table where Miss Smith and Shelley Carter were sitting. Shelley was speaking.

"I'm doing what I can, but he needs a proper swimming coach."

"Hello, Miss Smith!" KC said as they walked past.

Miss Smith didn't look very pleased to see them. "Hello," she said grumpily, turning back to Shelley Carter.

Chapter 7
Good Work, Sam

When Poppy got home, Sam was jumping up and down with excitement.

"Hi, Sam. How was the class trip to the dinosaur museum? Looks like you had a great time!"

"The museum was brilliant. I thought it was going to be just old bones, but it was much more exciting than that."

"What, real dinosaurs?"

"Very funny. No, but they had these life-size models that looked like real dinosaurs. They moved too, and made dinosaur noises. There was this T-Rex with blood dripping down from its teeth!

But it's not the museum that I'm excited about. It's what I saw on the way home!"

"What did you see?"

"I saw Rob Smith!"

"Wow! Where?"

"On our way back to school. Our bus got held up outside Longmead School – you know, the high school on the other side of town. We just got there when all the kids were pouring out, so everything got jammed up. I saw Rob Smith waiting outside for the school bus with a whole lot of other guys."

"Are you sure it was him?"

"Yes. He was wearing that cap he pulls down over his face. I remembered the badge that was on it. Only this time I could see his face. And he was carrying that sports bag. You've got to be good at noticing things if you're going to be a detective, you know!"

"So he goes to Longmead School. I'll phone KC and tell her," said Poppy running to tell her friend.

"KC. Sam's done it again - he's found out that Rob Smith goes to Longmead."

"That's great! My cousin, Ryan, goes to Longmead. He's about the same age as Rob Smith. I'll see if I can find out anything from him!"

Poppy, Sam and KC were at the pool early the next morning. Once again, they could hear the sound of swimming inside the pool.

"I phoned Ryan last night," KC told them. "He knows who Rob Smith is, but he doesn't know too much about him. He said Rob only started at the school this term, and he's friendly with a boy called Jimmy. Ryan thought I was interested in boys! I didn't want to tell him anything."

Sam was looking around the car park, but there was no sign of Miss Smith; just a blue car with a man and a woman sitting inside it.

"She probably only picks him up when it rains," said KC.

"Hey, listen," Sam said. "The splashing stopped. Rob must have finished. Let's watch for him."

They saw him coming out. Poppy moved away, in case KC jabbed her in the ribs again.

"Why don't we go talk to him?" KC asked.

 "He'd probably be grumpy, just like Miss Smith was."

Just then, the two people in the car got out. The man had a camera around his neck. They walked up to Rob Smith and the man started to take photographs. The woman pushed a voice recorder towards Rob Smith's face and started questioning him.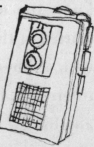

It was obvious that Rob Smith didn't want to talk to them.

They could hear him shouting.  He pushed the voice recorder away, but the man kept on taking photographs. Rob turned and threw his sports bag at the man with the camera, which almost knocked him over. Then Rob ran out of the gate, with the man and woman chasing him.

"They'll never catch him," KC said.

They went over to the sports bag, which was lying on the ground. It had burst open and bits and pieces had spilled out – school books, swimming gear – and a badge.

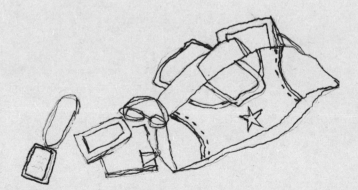

"What should we do with this?" asked KC.

"Let's hand it in at the reception desk. If we

leave it, that man and woman will take it," said Poppy.

"Who do you think they were?" asked KC.

"Newspaper reporters," said Poppy. "There really is a mystery going on here! Who can Rob Smith be?"

Sam had been busy picking everything up and putting it back in the bag. The plastic badge was on a long chain and had a photograph.

"Hey!" Sam said. "This is a really big clue!"

"What?"

"The badge has Rob's picture, but his name isn't Rob Smith!"

Chapter 8
Tackling Shelley

Poppy and KC crowded around to read what was on the badge.

NATIONAL SWIMMING ACADEMY
Rob Towers

And there was his picture.

"Who's Rob Towers?" asked KC.

"Don't know. But that picture's definitely the secret swimmer!"

"Quick!" said Sam. "Before those reporters come back. Let's get into the sports centre."

They rushed inside with the bag. They were just about to hand it in at the main desk when they saw Shelley Carter looking at the notice board.

Poppy went over to her. "Please, Miss Carter, I think you should have this."

She looked carefully at Shelley Carter's face. "Rob Towers dropped it in the car park."

Shelley Carter gasped and looked at Poppy, but just then Mrs. Hardiman arrived. Poppy handed over the bag, and she and KC went to change.

Sam couldn't wait to get on the internet to find out more about Rob Towers, but it was a frustrating day at school. It was sunny, so his class teacher wouldn't let him stay in at break time to surf the web.

At last it was time to go home. KC went to Poppy's house so they could work together on a school project. Sam rushed to the computer and typed in 'Rob Towers Swimmer'. The first result was what he wanted.

"Got him! Look at this!"

The first web page was about a swimming event a few months earlier. Sam printed out the page. Poppy and KC tried to read it as it came out of the printer.

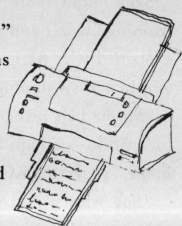

Poppy read the page out aloud.

"The gold medal in the freestyle event was won by fourteen year old Rob Towers. Rob, who is trained by national coach Michelle Hardy, is seen as one of the most promising swimmers in the country."

"Look at the picture," Sam said. "It's definitely him."

Poppy was reading on.

"It says here that Rob lives in Weston," she

said. "That's miles from here."

Sam found more web pages showing Rob winning medals and trophies, but nothing that explained why he had come to their town, or why he was swimming in secret.

"Maybe he's just come to stay with his aunt for a while – perhaps he's got family problems at home," suggested KC.

"But why would the newspapers want to photograph him?" said Poppy.

Then KC had a good idea. "Sam, search for his coach – what's her name? Michelle Hardy."

Sam typed in 'Michelle Hardy swimming'.

"Michelle Hardy, national swimming coach. It's a news report. I'll print it. out."

KC read the report as the paper churned out of the printer.

SETBACK FOR NATIONAL SQUAD

Michelle Hardy, the swimming coach for the national junior team, has been forced to pull out of all coaching after discovering she is suffering from a serious illness. Michelle was a popular and highly effective coach, and the news has come as a terrible shock to the members of the team.

It has been announced that Todd Drake, Olympic silver medallist, will take over from Michelle as the squad's new coach.

"What's the date on that?" Poppy asked.

"About three months ago."

"Well, that doesn't help," Poppy said. It's all still a mystery."

Just then Poppy's mum came to the door. "Poppy, there's a woman named Shelley Carter, from the sports centre, on the telephone. She'd like to talk to you."

The three friends looked at each other. Were they in trouble?

"Hello?"

"Hello Poppy. Mrs. Hardiman gave me your phone number. I'd like to talk to you about what happened this morning. Would your parents mind if I came round to talk to you? It's important. I can be there in ten minutes."

Poppy nervously called out to her mum.

"Mum, would it be all right if Shelley Carter came round to talk to us? She says it's important."

Poppy's mum was puzzled. "What can be so important that it can't wait until you go to the sports centre? I suppose it's all right, but KC has to go home soon."

Poppy picked up the phone again.

"Mum says that's fine. See you soon," she said, puzzled.

Chapter 9
Much Worse

When Shelley Carter arrived, she smiled at all of them, and patted Jasper, who had come to check out the stranger coming in to his house. Jasper decided that Shelley Carter was harmless, and trotted back to his warm basket in the kitchen.

"I'm glad you're all here," Shelley Carter said and turned to Poppy's mum. "Thank you so much for letting me talk to them. It's important! Please stay and listen if you would like to."

Shelley took out a little notebook.

"Thank you for bringing in Rob's bag this morning. Would you tell me everything that happened?"

"It's Rob Tower's bag, isn't it?" said Poppy.

"Yes. I wondered how you knew who he was, but I realised that you'd probably seen his badge. Please promise not to tell anyone about him. I know that Rob was talking to some people in the car park. One of the other lifeguards saw. Do you know who they were?"

"We're sure they were newspaper reporters," answered KC. "We couldn't hear what they said, but they were taking photographs and trying to interview him. Rob got angry and threw the bag at the cameraman, and then ran off. The reporters chased him."

Shelley sighed. "I thought they'd find him sooner or later."

Poppy was puzzled. "Please tell us what's going on. We promise not to tell anyone."

"I will. You all deserve it. What do you know about Rob Towers?"

Sam showed her the printouts they had from the internet.

"We got interested because we heard him swimming in the morning before the sports centre opened," he said. "We sneaked in and watched him and found out he was a brilliant swimmer. His aunt, Miss Smith who teaches at our school, wouldn't tell us anything about him."

"You three are great detectives," Shelley said. "I just hope you don't become newspaper reporters! So, you know Miss Smith is Rob's aunt. Rob is a member of the national swimming team. He's probably the best swimmer of his age in the country. The trouble is he's not very confident about it. Any little setback and he starts saying he's no good, and he's going to give up.

"He had an excellent coach, Michelle Hardy, who was building his confidence, so he was winning medals. Everything was going well, until Michelle Hardy became ill."

"What happened then?" asked Poppy.

"A new coach called Todd Drake came. He was a champion swimmer, and a good coach, but he didn't understand Rob. Todd thought the best way to coach Ron was to tell him he wasn't good enough, and that he had to do better. Rob finally walked out. He left the squad and said he was going to give up swimming competitions.

"Everyone was upset, especially Rob's parents. Then the newspapers found out that Rob had stopped going to the coaching. They started hanging around his house to get him to talk.

"Rob's parents decided that Rob would move here for a while, and stay with his aunt, away the newspapers. This would give him a breathing space so he could think about his future. Miss Smith organised a place for him at Longmead School, using her name. So, while he was here he became Rob Smith."

"And now he's decided to swim again!" KC said. "Are you his coach, now?"

Shelley smiled and shook her head.

"I'm not good enough for that!" she laughed. "I'm really just a lifeguard at the sports centre, though I do some teaching for the very young children. The manager of the sports centre, Mr Tyler, is a friend of Miss Smith's. When Rob decided he would like to do some swimming again, just to keep in practice, she asked him. So my boss let me into the secret and asked me if I would act as lifeguard for extra early morning sessions. Only a few people at the sports centre know who Rob really is. It was all going so well – until now."

Shelley sighed. "I've no idea how the newspapers managed to find out where Rob is.

"It's sad, but Rob doesn't get on too well with his aunt, and Rob began to trust me as a friend. I just hope he doesn't blame me for what happened."

"Is Rob going to give up swimming again? Just because the reporters found out where he is? He was really very angry with them," said Poppy.

"I'm afraid it's worse than that," Shelley said. "Rob didn't go home this afternoon. And he wasn't in school today. He's disappeared!"

Chapter 10

A postcard

The next morning, Poppy and KC had a surprise at school. Miss Smith came to talk to them privately.

"I want to apologise for the way I spoke to you the other day. I was grateful that you found Rob's chain, and I know I didn't show it."

Poppy and KC weren't used to having teachers apologise!

"That's all right," Poppy said. "We know now why you didn't want to talk about Rob."

"Shelley Carter told me she'd spoken to you. Thank you for letting her know what happened yesterday morning."

"Has Rob come home yet?"

Miss Smith looked worried. "No, I'm afraid not. I've told his parents, of course, and the police. The last thing anyone wanted was for all this to get into the newspapers but, unless we find him soon, we'll have to have a public appeal. That would ruin everything."

"We'll do everything we can to help," said Poppy.

Miss Smith smiled. She didn't think that two young girls would be much help in tracking him down, though she didn't say so.

"Thank you very much. I'll give you my address and phone number, just in case you see anything, or remember anything else about yesterday."

Poppy and KC went to find Sam and told him what had happened.

"We've got to find him," said Poppy. "He's probably hiding somewhere, really upset. It'll ruin any chance of him becoming a great swimmer."

"I don't know what we can do," said KC. "We don't have any clues."

"Yes, we do," said Poppy. "Do you remember that friend of Rob's at Longmead school – can you remember what his name was?"

"Jimmy, I think," said KC. "I'll phone my cousin tonight!"

Ryan promised he would see what he could find out from Jimmy.

At coaching the next morning, there was no sign of Rob. At the end of the session, Poppy and KC met Sam, in the lobby. They were just heading off to school when Shelley Carter rushed up to them.

"Hello," Poppy said. "Has Rob been found?"

"No, but he sent a postcard – look!"

Poppy took it. It showed an old brown coloured picture of a village, taken many years ago.

Some people were sitting in a horse drawn carriage, staring at the camera with serious faces. They all wore old-fashioned clothes, and the men were even wearing top hats.

Poppy turned the card over and read it.

'Don't worry, Shelley, I'm OK.' it said. 'Tell Aunt Jill not to try to find me. I need to think things through. Sorry to be a pain. See you, Rob.'

"I tried to phone Miss Smith at home but she'd already left for school. Would you take the card with you, and give it to her?"

"Of course," said Poppy.

On the way to school, they all looked at the postcard for clues.

Then KC had a good idea.

"You know that shop on the way to school – the one that sells everything – newspapers, groceries, sweets – all that stuff?"

"What about it?" said Sam.

"It's got a sign in the window about photocopying. We can make a copy of the card before we give it to Miss Smith."

They copied sides of the postcard.

When they got to school, they knocked on the staff room door and asked for Miss Smith. She looked tired and worried.

"Shelley Carter got this card this morning at the sports centre. She tried to phone you but you had already left for work, so she asked us to bring it to school."

Miss Smith took the card and read it. She looked both relieved and annoyed.

"Thank you very much. As you can see, it's good news."

She went into the staff room and shut the door.

"I'm not surprised Rob sent the card to Shelley Carter. She's nice and he trusted her. Miss Smith is grumpy," said KC.

Chapter 11

Looking for Jimmy

At lunchtime, they found a quiet place to look at the photocopies.

"The postmark is from here, so he can't be far away. It was sent yesterday," Poppy said.

"What do you think these blobs are?" Sam said.

There were four dark blobs on the back of the postcard, one on each corner.

"The postcard was probably stuck in something," said KC.

They looked at the picture on the front of the card.

"Looks about a million years old," Sam mused. "I'm surprised there aren't any dinosaurs in it!"

"Probably about a hundred years," said Poppy.

"But where is it? That might be an important clue."

"I don't know. But wherever it is, I don't suppose it looks like that now. No one wears hats like that now."

That evening, KC got a phone call from her cousin Ryan.

"Hi, KC. Did you know Rob Smith's disappeared? Turns out he was a famous swimmer or something!"

"Ryan, who told you that?" asked KC.

"A friend of mine has a friend who's friends with Jimmy, who Rob Smith was friendly with. Only his name wasn't Rob Smith. What do you know about all this? Do you know who he is?"

KC tried to follow what Ryan had said. She thought she'd better not tell him who Rob Smith really was and tried to change the subject.

"Do you know what Jimmy's second name is?"

"Yes. I told you my friend's a friend of a friend of his. This friend – not my friend, Jimmy's friend – was working with Jimmy and Rob on a local history project. Jimmy's name is Robbins – Jimmy Robbins. People have been asking him

64

about Rob but he won't tell them anything. He just gets really mad and storms off – no idea why. Hey, KC, you do know something about this Rob, don't you? Come on! Everyone at school wants to know."

"Sorry, Ryan; have to go. Catch you later," said KC, hurriedly.

KC called Poppy.

"Jimmy's last name is Robbins. He and Rob were working on a local history project. That might be where he got the postcard from. Oh, and bad news. Ryan knows that Rob has disappeared!"

"How does he know that?"

"He's got a friend who's got a friend who . . . oh, never mind, he just does. But he doesn't know who Rob really is. But he knows I know. So I think we need to find Rob as soon as possible, before everybody else knows!"

Sam was listening to Poppy's conversation. When she put down the phone, she saw he was looking through the phone book.

"What are you doing?"

"Looking for people named Robbins who live around here."

"There's lots." He started counting. "Eighteen!"

"It's not going to be easy. We can't just phone everyone to ask if they've got someone called Jimmy living there," said Poppy.

"I guess not."

Sam picked up the photocopy of the postcard.

"Maybe there's a clue here. Rob and Jimmy were doing a project on local history. Maybe this is the village that Jimmy lives in, but one hundred years ago."

"That's a good idea, Sam! Let's ask Mum and Dad if they know where it is."

But neither of them recognised where the photo was taken.

"If you think the card shows a place near here, why don't you go to the library?" suggested their dad. "There's a section on local history. I'm sure you'd be able to find out. Why do you need to know, anyway?"

"Just a project we're working on," said Poppy. She knew adults were always fooled when she said that! "Thanks Dad; the library's a really good idea. Mum, tomorrow's Friday and it's not swimming club. Can you pick us up from the library, instead, please?"

KC's family went to a movie after school on Friday, so Poppy and Sam walked down to the library by themselves. They asked the woman at the desk where they might find information on local history.

"We have a local history reference section upstairs. If you need any help, ask Emma."

When they got to the Local History section they found a lot more than books. An elderly man was sitting at the table, looking through a file of old papers with a magnifying glass. There were drawers with labels, saying things like 'maps' and 'council planning reports.'

Sam saw a section marked 'postcards', with lots of small drawers. Poppy pulled one out. It was full of old postcards of the town.

"This one shows the High Street! Look at those old cars! And look what these kids are wearing," she said.

"Hello, you two! Can I help you?"

"Hello," said Poppy. "Are you Emma? The woman at the desk said you might be able to help us."

"Yes, I'm Emma. I'll do my best to help. What do you want to know?"

Poppy showed her the photocopy of the old postcard.

"We're trying to find out where this. We know it's somewhere near here, but it's probably changed since it was taken."

Emma looked at the picture.

"This could be difficult," she said. "All of

the postcards are filed under the name of the street or village where the picture was taken. You would have to look through all of them to find a matching one. And we've got thousands of them!"

This was really bad news.

"I don't think we've got time for that. Our mum is picking us up soon. Thank you for your help, though."

"May I help? I've lived around here all my life," said a voice. The elderly man got up from his desk and came over. "May I have a look?"

He peered at the photocopy through tiny glasses. "Oh yes, this is Stockton village! That house in the background is still there."

"Thank you very much!" Poppy said, excitedly. "That's just what we needed to know!"

Emma went to a drawer and looked through

the postcards.

"These are our Stockton cards. Look! I've found a copy of your card."

The picture was exactly the same and, on the back, in neat writing, it said 'Horse and Carriage at Stockton village, 1907.'

Poppy and Sam went downstairs to wait for their mum.

"That's brilliant!" Poppy said. "I can't wait to tell KC."

"But where's Stockton?" asked Sam.

"It's outside town, where the hills start. I went there for a party once," Poppy remembered.

As soon as they got home, Sam looked through the phone book again.

"I've found it!" he said. "Look! Robbins, A J. Duck House, Main Street, Stockton. Phone number is – "

"Sam, we just can't phone them up," said Poppy. What would we say if that happened to us? Anyway, you heard what KC's cousin said. If you talk about Rob to Jimmy, he just gets mad and storms off. But I bet he knows something."

"What will we do?"

"Not sure. But KC should be home by now. I'll phone her. She might have some ideas."

Just then the phone rang. It was KC. She couldn't wait to find out what had happened at the library.

Over supper, Poppy asked about the fun run.

"Mum, Shelley Carter's organising a fun run at Stockton tomorrow. Can we go, please? And can we take Jasper?"

"I don't see why not. All this swimming and, now, running! You are going to be fit!"

After supper Poppy rang KC and told her about the fun run.

"That's cool! I'm sure Mum will let me come! Hang on, Poppy, and I'll go ask!"

Poppy heard KC rushing off. A minute later she was back again.

"Mum says yes! Great!"

The next day was cold, but sunny. Poppy had been worried that, if it rained, the fun run would be called off.

Poppy's dad was taking them to Stockton, and mum was picking them up at the end of the day

The three friends were all warmly dressed in tracksuits. There were a lot of cars in the small car park at Stockton, and more cars were parked along the road.

Dad weaved the car through the traffic to the village green.

They scrambled out of the car. Jasper was really excited by all the crowds, and kept tugging at his lead.

"Be careful!" called their dad, as the three friends headed for the village green. "And good luck!"

Flags had been stuck in the ground in the middle of the green, to mark the start and finish. A man with a loud speaker was trying to organise everyone, but nobody seemed to be listening to him.

"There's Shelley Carter," Poppy said, giving KC a nudge in the ribs, for a change. "She's wearing her sports centre red tracksuit."

Sam started to cross the village green to where Shelley was standing, but Poppy pulled him back.

"We've got twenty minutes before the race starts," she said. "There's just enough time for us to do a bit of exploring."

"It's a big village," Sam said. "It's going to take ages to find the house."

"Shouldn't do," said KC. "Duck House is in Main Street. That's bound to be in the middle of the village, near this green."

Poppy was looking along a row of old houses. She pointed.

"A sign – Main Street! Over there! And I'm sure that's the house that's in the photograph!"

Chapter 13

Keep Going!

Sam pulled the photocopy of the postcard out of his pocket.

"You're right, and it hasn't changed much."

They walked over to look at the house. It wasn't Duck Cottage, though – it was called Mill House.

"I bet there used to be an old mill near here," KC said. "Look at that stream. There was probably a mill wheel, going round and round grinding corn."

"Duck Cottage is near here," Sam said.

"How do you know?"

Sam pointed at the busy stream, chuckling under a road bridge. Jasper stuck his nose over the bridge. Water! He was getting thirsty!

"Where do you find ducks?" said Sam.

Just then, the noise of chattering on the green started to die down. The man with the loudspeaker had gotten everyone's attention at last!

"The fun run will be starting in ten minutes!" The voice boomed. "Anyone who has not registered to take part must do so now, at the registration desk!"

"Come on, quick!" Poppy said. "I'd forgotten we had to do that! Come on, Jasper!"

The three rushed across to the green, tugging at Jasper. There was a desk set up, with people taking the names of runners. Shelley Carter was helping.

"Hi Shelley!" Poppy said.

"Hi Poppy, Hi KC, Hi Sam, Hi dog. Really glad you could make it!" Shelley said.

"Any news on you-know-who?" KC asked.

Shelley shook her head. "'Afraid not. We'll follow up your idea, just in case. Meet you here after the fun run – if you're not too exhausted!"

"Great!" said Poppy. "See you then!"

At last everyone was ready to start, though it

was a lot more than ten minutes later!

"He just said that to hurry everyone up!" Sam said.

The race really was going to be fun. Most people wore tracksuits because it was cold, but some wore running kits. They stood around with goose bumps wishing the race would get going. Some people wore costumes. One man was dressed as a duck!

"I wonder if he lives at Duck Cottage," Sam whispered.

Some yelled "GO!" into the megaphone, and everyone started running. The best runners were soon out in front. Most people were taking part just for fun or to raise money, and they just jogged along, laughing and talking. Poppy and KC took turns to run with Jasper. He enjoyed the race, but he was determined to tangle his lead around the legs of the person running with him.

The run soon left the village and was in the countryside. The ground was too muddy for the race to go into fields, so the route ran down small roads that had been closed to traffic. All along the route, there were pink and yellow balloons to show the way, though everyone just had to follow the crowd.

Sam wasn't as fast as the two girls and Jasper.

"Slow down," he grumbled. "It's a fun run, not a race, and it's not much fun trying to keep up with you three!"

There were marshals in yellow jackets in case anyone got into trouble. Their main job seemed to be waving at everyone as they ran past.

MAIN STREET

The route was
a big circle, so the
finish line was back on
the village green. At one point,
near a wood, they saw a sign saying
'Half way – keep going!'

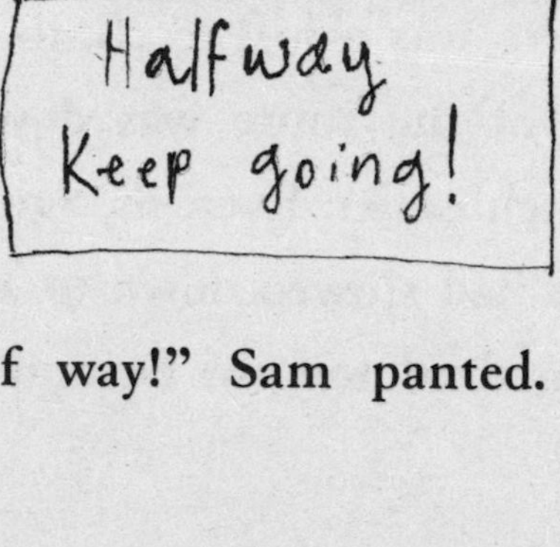

Halfway
Keep going!

"Only half way!" Sam panted. "My legs hurt."

Lots of people stopped for a rest. Not everyone was very fit. Two marshals were giving out free bottles of water. Sam, Poppy and KC shared a bottle. Jasper was thirsty, too, and the organisers had put bowls of water on the roadside for all the dogs.

"Come on, Jasper!" Poppy said. "You must have had enough to drink by now! Come on, everyone! Only half the race left to do!"

The first half of the race had been hard work because there was a hill to climb. On the way, back most of the route was downhill, which made it much easier. Even so, Sam was finding it hard. He had slowed down to a walk. Jasper was getting tired too, so he and Sam walked together.

KC was still full of energy. She was rushing on ahead.

"Slow down, KC!" Poppy said. "I've got to watch Sam and Jasper!"

At last, the village green was in sight. The organisers had special silver blankets for anyone who was cold, but only a few people needed these. A band was playing, and food stalls had been set up all over the green. Sam flopped down on the ground.

"Come on Sam. We've got to find Shelley."

Sam groaned. "Whatever."

They didn't need to hunt for Shelley – she found them first.

"Hi gang. How was the run?"

"I'm exhausted," Sam said. "It's all right for you, you didn't have to run. That's why you're not tired!"

"Didn't run? Of course I did! I passed you while you were all guzzling water at the half-way point. I've been back for ages!"

"Right, I've finished here. Would you like a

healthy burger before we go looking for Duck Cottage?"

"Yummy!"

The three friends didn't usually eat burgers, but they had used a lot of energy and were very hungry. There was even one for Jasper.

Sam explained his idea about the stream and the ducks, so they started the search back at Mill House.

"We could split up to look," KC suggested.

"I've got a better idea," Shelley said, and went up to a family walking back from the race.

"Excuse me, we're looking for Duck Cottage. Can you help?"

"That's easy," said one of the children. "It's just three doors down! Mr and Mrs Robbins, Sarah and Jimmy live there."

Duck Cottage had a small front garden and a passage at the side, leading round to the back of the house.

"What now?" KC asked.

"I'm going to knock on the door and ask to

see Jimmy," Shelley said. "We can't go sneaking around."

"Grown-ups are sensible," Poppy thought. "Though sneaking around would be more fun!"

They went up the short path to the front door and rang the bell. But nothing happened. Shelley rang again, but it was clear there was nobody in.

"I think we're going to have to give up," Shelly said. "I'll phone them tonight."

Then they heard a loud quacking of ducks, and a barking, and it came from the back of the house.

Chapter 14

Ducks are Fun!

It was no one's fault. Sam had been holding Jasper's lead, but not tight enough. Jasper's ears had pricked up. Ducks! They were fun to chase! He'd dashed towards the sound of the ducks, barking like mad.

"Jasper! Come back!" Poppy yelled, but Jasper took no notice.

"We'd better go after him," Shelley said. "We won't be very popular if he kills and eats one of the Robbins' ducks."

They all rushed after Jasper. The back garden of Duck Cottage was much bigger than the front. There  was a large lawn and in the middle of it was a duck pond.

Jasper was standing at the edge of the pond, barking furiously at four ducks. The ducks didn't seem to be worried at all.

Poppy grabbed Jasper's lead and started to pull him away from the pond.

KC looked around the garden. What a large garden! There was a small wood to one side; on the other side, there was a shed.

Just then, something moved. Someone was looking out of the window of the shed! She couldn't see who it as, but she knew that baseball cap!

"Shelley! Poppy!" she whispered. "It's Rob!

He's down there, in that shed! Look!"

"By the time they looked, the face had disappeared. Shelley walked over to the shed and tapped gently on the door.

"Rob, it's me, Shelley."

The door opened slowly, and out came a sad-looking Rob.

When Rob had looked out of the window, he had been amazed to see what was happening outside. A hairy dog was barking at the ducks, two girls and a boy that he'd never seen before were trying to pull him away, and Shelley Carter, whom he knew very well, was with them! He'd pulled back, hoping they hadn't seen him. When he heard the tap on the door and heard Shelley's voice, he knew they had.

"Hello, Shelley. How did you know where I was?"

But there wasn't time for explanations. The Robbins family were just arriving home – and they were very surprised to find their garden full of people and a barking dog!

"What is going on?" Mr Robbins demanded. "Who are you? What are you doing in our garden?"

Rob looked at Jimmy, who knew just a little bit more than his parents – though he didn't know who these other people were.

"Sorry, Jimmy," Rob said. "This is Shelley, from the sports centre. I don't know who these three are, and I don't know how Shelley knew I was here."

Mrs Robbins noticed that Rob looked cold – he was beginning to shiver.

"Well, it sounds as if we all need to go inside and talk this through," she said. Come on, everyone – and don't forget to wipe your feet please!"

Soon everyone was indoors, drinking hot chocolate and eating cake. Jimmy tried to explain what had been going on.

"Mum, Dad, this is Rob – Rob Towers, the famous swimmer. We've been friends since he came to Longmead a few months ago. Rob's had a really bad time, and then the newspapers starting chasing him. He needed to get away for a bit."

"Rob Towers!" Jimmy's dad said. "There was something about you on the local radio this afternoon. They said you'd disappeared, and everyone was worried. The police have been hunting for you! Surely you haven't been living in that cold shed all this time?"

"No," said Rob. "I stayed in Jimmy's bedroom most of the time. I hid in the closet when you came in. I only went down to the shed today because it was the weekend and you were all here. I didn't want you to find me."

Sarah, Jimmy's sister, spoke next.

"So that was why you put that 'keep out' sign on your bedroom door, Jimmy! I thought you were just being mean to me!"

Shelley introduced herself and explained how

she was involved.

"I had no idea where Rob was. It was these three children who did the detective work and tracked him down."

Poppy and KC thought that Rob might be angry, and were relieved to find that he wasn't.

"It was fine in the week in Jimmy's room, but I've had a miserable, cold day in the shed. I'd decided to go back to my aunt's this evening. anyway. I've had time to think about things, and I realised just how stupid I've been. Everyone must have been really worried."

Shelley phoned Miss Smith to tell her that Rob was fine, and asked her to tell the police.

Then Poppy looked at her watch.

"Come on; it's time to meet KC's mother! Thanks for the drinks, Mrs Robbins." She turned to Rob.

"Rob, I hope everything works out OK for you. You are a really great swimmer, you know."

Rob smiled at her.

"Thanks," he said. It's great to know that

people care enough to look for me. But I haven't decided about swimming yet."

They left the Robbins' house and went out into the Village Street. It was almost dark, and street lights were beginning to glow. It was a cold evening; too cold too be sitting in a garden shed.

Rob went with Shelley, who was going to take him home in her car.

"Here's your mum, now, KC," Poppy said. "On time as usual!"

"Have you had a good day?" KC's mum asked.

Had they? They had so much to tell her it was hard to know where to start!

Chapter 15

Not Looking Good

Morning swimming practice got more serious as the competition approached.

Poppy, KC and the two boys, Rick and Jerry, were improving all the time, and Mrs. Hardiman was sure they would do well.

It was the first practice after their adventure in Stockton. Mrs. Hardiman started the session with a team talk.

"As you know, the competition is next Saturday. Luckily for us, it's taking place here, so we're on home ground! There are six teams competing. There will be freestyle, breaststroke and backstroke events. There are separate races for boys and girls, but the relay race at the end is mixed — all four of you are in that. Today, we're going to work on change-overs for the relay race. It's very easy to go too soon, and then you get disqualified. Don't forget — the judges are very good at spotting that!"

"Who are the judges?"

"I'm one, and Shelley Carter will help. You know her, don't you?"

"Yes, we do!" KC said.

After the practice session Poppy, KC and Sam went to find Shelley.

"What's the news on Rob?" asked Poppy.

"Well, he's safely at home with Miss Smith. He hasn't gone back to school yet, but he'll be back there next week."

"What about the newspaper people?"

"Good news: I told Miss Smith what they did outside the Sports Centre, and she complained to the paper. Reporters aren't allowed to interview young people without permission from an adult. So that won't happen again."

"What about Rob's swimming?" asked KC. "He said he was still thinking about that."

"I don't know," Shelley said. "But I'm keeping my fingers crossed. Rob's parents have been in touch with the national team, and they would really like him to start training again.

The trouble is, as you know, he doesn't do well with the new coach."

"Why doesn't he stay here?" Poppy asked. "Mrs. Hardiman could train him – she's a great coach!"

Shelley smiled. "I know she is. But there's a big difference between what we can do here, and the training the national team gets. If he's going to be a champion, he needs to get back there soon."

The team had an extra morning practice that week because of the competition on Saturday. The girls and Sam had hoped to hear the sound of splashing when they arrived for the sessions, but there was only silence.

"It's not looking good," Poppy said. "I think Rob's going to give up. What a shame!"

"It's the reporters' fault!" said KC.

As Saturday came closer, KC and Poppy almost forgot about Rob. They were too busy thinking about the swimming competition. They were really looking forward to it, but they both felt very nervous. Lots of people would be coming to watch – all the families of the people taking part. What if they did something wrong, like getting disqualified for going too soon? And what if they did really badly and let Mrs Hardiman down? After all, the other teams might be really good – as good as Rob!

The night before the race, Poppy couldn't sleep. There was a fluttery feeling in her tummy. She knew it was just nerves, but knowing that didn't help much. She decided she wasn't looking forward to the competition at all. Why had she let herself be talked into it? Swimming was fun, so why spoil it by going in for competitions?

What would people say though, if she dropped out now? She thought of all the people she would let down – her parents, KC, Mrs. Hardiman.

She had to do it. Not just for those people, but for herself. Then Poppy thought about Rob.

What had he decided to do? Lying there, she knew exactly what he must have felt when he decided to give everything up. Well, whatever he decided, she wasn't going to give up. And, with that thought, she fell asleep.

Chapter 16
Come On, Poppy!

Saturday was cold and miserable, but that didn't matter. It wasn't a fun run – swimming was indoors!

There were lots of cars outside the pool when Poppy and KC arrived. Lots of families were arriving for the competition.

"Just go out there and enjoy yourself," Mrs. Hardiman said. "I'm sure you'll do really well but, if you don't, it's not the end of the world. It's the fun of taking part that counts, and trying your best. Whatever happens, your families and I will be really proud of you."

There were twelve boys and twelve girls, too many to race together, so the first races would be heats with six swimmers in each heat. The fastest three would go through to the final. KC was worried about the backstroke event. She really wasn't very good at backstroke. Poppy was, though, so maybe she would do well in this event.

Everyone was changed and ready. All the swimmers wore a coloured armband to show what team they were in. Poppy looked across to the other teams, and saw someone she knew.

"Hey, KC, look. It's Angie!"

They had met Angie last term, when they went to dancing class. She went to a school in the next town.

"Hi Angie! I didn't know you were a swimmer!"

"Hi, Poppy! Hi, KC! I'll tell you a secret. I'm the team substitute! Charlotte let us down at the last minute – got panicked. That's why I'm here!"

Poppy thought about the feelings she'd had last night. She had felt panicked, too, but she was going through with it. That made her feel good.

A whistle blew. It was the

first heat for the girls' freestyle race. Freestyle meant you could choose how you swam, but most people used the front crawl. Crawl didn't sound very fast, but it was the fastest of all the strokes. Poppy was pleased. This was her best event, but she had to wait until the second heat; KC was swimming in this one.

"On your marks, get set…" BANG!

Each race was two lengths of the pool. Would KC make a good turn? Most of the time she did, but sometimes she messed up.

"Come on KC! You can do it!"

Nearer and nearer to the end of the pool. KC got ready for the turn – but left it too late! With a scramble she was round, but she had lost a couple of seconds.

"Go for it, KC!" yelled Poppy.

KC wasn't the only one who had made a bad turn, so she was still in with a chance. Desperately, she managed to push herself forward.

"Third place! Well done, KC!"

KC was still in with a chance of the final, but all the swimmers in the next race would have to be slower – and she didn't think that was likely, especially with Poppy swimming!

She started to climb out of the pool. Each lane had a judge who was taking the time on a stopwatch. She looked up – and nearly fell back into the pool!

"Rob! Are you one of the judges?"

"Rob smiled. "Hi – KC, isn't it? Yes, Shelley roped me in to help. Guess I just can't stay away from swimming pools."

Now it was Poppy's heat. KC put on her tracksuit top. She had heard Poppy cheering for her. Now she was going to cheer for Poppy.

BANG! The starter's gun echoed around the pool.

A perfect start from Poppy. She was in the lead on the first length. How would she manage the turn?

"Come on Poppy! You can do it!" called KC.

In the viewing gallery, KC could see Sam, and Poppy's mum and dad, leaping up and down with excitement.

"Go, Poppy! Good turn!"

Poppy was well in the lead now. No one was going to beat her. Three yards, two, one – she touched, and the judges' stopwatches clicked. Loud cheers and screams reverberated around the poolside.

The times were put up on the board. A girl from the first heat called Melanie had the fastest time. Poppy was second, but it was close. It was going to be a tough final!

Poppy and KC had a break now because it was time for the boys' freestyle heats. Rick came in last in his heat, but Jerry squeezed into the final with the third best time.

Poppy and KC really wanted to chat to Rob,

but he was much too busy with his timekeeping. Anyway, it might not look good talking to one of the judges!

Soon, it was time for the girls' breaststroke. Both girls were okay at this, but they ended up disappointed; neither of them got into the final. Angie managed to get the second best time – she was a better swimmer than Poppy and KC had thought.

The next event was the backstroke. Poppy didn't think she had much chance at this, but she was sure KC would be great.

KC was in the first heat this time. Because it was the backstroke, the swimmers started in the water. KC got off to a great start, and just kept going. But would the turn let her down this time?

"Go, KC!"

The turn was perfect. KC was well ahead in the second length, and won easily. There was no one in the second heat that could beat her – she had the best time!

The boys' backstroke heats were disappointing. Jerry got disqualified in his heat for jumping the gun. Rick was just too slow.

But who would win the all-important relay race?

Chapter 17

The Surprise Celebrity

There was a break after the heats, so that all the swimmers could get their breath back in time for the finals. The afternoon would end with the relay race, with everyone involved.

KC and Poppy saw Rob talking to Shelley, and went over.

"Don't ask him about swimming," Poppy hissed to KC. "He probably doesn't want to talk about it."

But Rob was quite happy to talk about it.

"Hi, you two detectives," he said. "I've just been telling Shelley that I've decided to go back to the national team. After all your hard work looking for me, I can't let you down, can I?"

"What about your coach, though?" KC asked.

Poppy groaned quietly to herself. That wasn't a tactful thing to say!

But Rob seemed relaxed about it.

"It's OK. I'm feeling better about things now. We'll just see how it works out. I'm sure it will be worth it in the end."

Someone called Rob over just then. When he'd gone Shelley whispered to the girls.

"Don't say anything, but Rob's going to get a big surprise at the end of the competition. Just wait and see!"

Poppy and KC wondered what she meant, but there wasn't time to think about it; the finals were starting.

The backstroke final was first. Because Mrs. Hardiman was a judge, she couldn't give KC any last minute advice, so she gave her a big wink, instead.

One of the other girls was as fast as KC, but her turn hadn't been great in the heat. This time her turn was perfect. Halfway down the last length she was an inch of two ahead of KC.

"Come on KC! You can do it!"

KC pushed. Hard. It was neck and neck when they touched the bar at the end. Who had got it?

The judges compared their watches. There was a long wait – then the announcement. KC had taken it – by a fraction of a second! KC and Poppy were both ecstatic.

Mrs. Hardiman's pupils, Rick and Jerry came second and fourth in the boys' breaststroke.

And then it was time for the girls' freestyle. All those butterflies started fluttering around in Poppy's tummy again as she walked up to her mark. She looked around. Rob was timing her lane!

Rob winked.

Bang! Poppy was off to a great start, but the girl who'd got the fastest time had a good start, too. Poppy pushed like mad, but gradually the other girl pulled ahead.

Poppy's turn was good, and for a few seconds she was ahead. Mrs. Hardiman had taught them well. Poppy could hear KC shouting for her, but she tried to shut everything out. Go. Go.

Melanie was in the lane next to Poppy. Gradually, she pulled ahead. There was nothing Poppy could do. Melanie first, Poppy second.

Poppy felt flattened and suddenly exhausted. She had wanted to win so much. But, as she climbed out of the pool, Rob was there, congratulating her.

"Poppy, that was brilliant. Second is great. You're a star!"

KC rushed up and gave Poppy a hug, just as Poppy had done when she had won. At least they hadn't let Mrs. Hardiman down.

After another break came the relay. Melanie's team won – she was obviously the best swimmer there today. Luckily for KC, she wasn't so good at backstroke. Poppy and KC's team came third, which meant they got a medal.

The judges started shifting things around at the end of the pool for the medal presentation.

They had three blocks, for first, second and third. All the swimmers had changed into tracksuits, and were lined up by the pool. Even the swimmers that hadn't won everything got a medal for taking part.

Mr. Tyler, the manager of the sports centre, started to speak through a microphone. He thanked everyone who had taken part, and all the judges, and all the grown ups who had worked hard to make it all happen.

"And now we come to the presentation of the awards," he said. "I am delighted to announce that we have a surprise celebrity to present this year's medals."

"I bet it's Rob!" Poppy whispered to KC.

But she was wrong.

"Ladies and gentleman, please welcome National Team Coach, Michelle Hardy!"

A woman in a tracksuit came through the door to the pool, her face beaming. There was a storm of applause, and she waved to everyone.

The medal ceremony was just a blur for Poppy and KC, but a wonderful blur. And afterwards, they watched with Shelley as Michelle went over to talk to Rob.

"Yes, Rob, I'm much better now, and I'm back. After Christmas, I'll be fit enough to take over again as head coach. Now, are you coming back? Are you up for it?"

Poppy couldn't help herself.

"Of course he is!" she shouted out, even though KC jabbed her in the ribs to shut her up.

And, of course, Poppy was absolutely right.

Three Together

If you've enjoyed meeting Poppy,
KC and Sam, you can try one of these
other exciting books in the
Three Together series.